W9-ANN-662

© 2004 by Barbour Publishing, Inc.

ISBN 1-59310-405-7

All rights reserved. No part of this publication may be reproduced or transmitted in any form or by any means without written permission of the publisher.

Scripture quotations are taken from the King James Version of the Bible.

Cover image © GettyOne

Published by Barbour Publishing, Inc., P.O. Box 719, Uhrichsville, Ohio 44683, www.barbourbooks.com

Our mission is to publish and distribute inspirational products offering exceptional value and biblical encouragement to the masses.

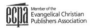
Member of the
Evangelical Christian
Publishers Association

Printed in China.
5 4 3 2 1

PEACE & GOODWILL

RACHEL QUILLIN

DayMaker
GREETING BOOKS

For unto you is born this day in the city of David a Saviour, which is Christ the Lord. And this shall be a sign unto you; Ye shall find the babe wrapped in swaddling clothes, lying in a manger. And suddenly there was with the angel a multitude of the heavenly host praising God, and saying, Glory to God in the highest, and on earth peace, good will toward men.

LUKE 2:11–14

The
PRINCE
of PEACE

For unto us a child is born, unto us a son is given:
and the government shall be upon his shoulder:
and his name shall be called Wonderful, Counsellor,
The mighty God, The everlasting Father,
The Prince of Peace.

ISAIAH 9:6

Kara arranged the last package under the tree and glanced at the clock—1:15 A.M. She sighed. She felt physically exhausted, but her mind was still going a hundred miles a minute, and she knew she'd never be able to sleep. A cup of hot cocoa would be nice anyway. She might as well relax and enjoy the beauty of the tree for a few minutes. After all, it wouldn't be long before three excited children would be tearing into the perfection.

As she looked around, Kara's gaze came to rest on the papier-mâché nativity scene she had made when she and Luke had first married. It wasn't as fancy as some of the store-bought sets, and she sometimes thought her camels looked more like dinosaurs. Still, the set was special. She had thought of replacing it but always changed her mind when she thought of the pleasure her children received in arranging the figures and acting out the Christmas story.

PEACE & GOODWILL

Her mind went back a week and a half to when her family had decorated for the holiday season. She could still see Molly, her seven-year-old daughter, as she placed Mary beside the manger and began to quietly sing a lullaby. Then Molly had repeated one of Kara's own bedtime phrases. "Sleep peacefully little one."

What could be more peaceful than a sleeping child? wondered Kara. When she tucked her babies into bed, she always felt such a gentle peace herself. Did Mary feel that same sense of peace as she tucked her child and Lord into his hay-filled cradle? What had the prophet Isaiah said this child would be named? The Prince of Peace. Certainly Mary must have been overwhelmed with peace—the peace only her child could bring.

For CHRIST is born of Mary,
　　　and gathered all ABOVE,
While mortals sleep, the ANGELS
　　　keep their watch of wondering LOVE.
O morning STARS together,
　　　proclaim the holy BIRTH,
And praises sing to GOD the King,
　　　and PEACE to men on earth!

PHILLIPS BROOKS, FROM "O LITTLE TOWN OF BETHLEHEM"

7

SILENT NIGHT

Silent night, holy night,
All is calm, all is bright
Round yon virgin mother and Child.
Holy Infant, so tender and mild,
Sleep in heavenly peace,
Sleep in heavenly peace.

Silent night, holy night,
Son of God, love's pure light;
Radiant beams from Thy holy face
With the dawn of redeeming grace,
Jesus, Lord, at Thy birth,
Jesus, Lord, at Thy birth.

JOSEF MOHR

PEACE & GOODWILL

First keep the

PEACE

WITHIN YOURSELF,

then you can also bring

PEACE

TO OTHERS.

THOMAS À KEMPIS

The LORD lift up

his countenance upon thee,

and give thee PEACE.

NUMBERS 6:26

INCARNATION
of PEACE

And the peace of God,
which passeth all understanding,
shall keep your hearts and minds through Christ Jesus.

PHILIPPIANS 4:7

Kara's thoughts shifted to the tiny figure of a baby in the manger. One of her favorite Christmas carols, "Away in a Manger," came to mind as she considered whom this figure represented. *Away in a manger, indeed,* thought Kara. She'd grown up on a farm and had seen what these feed troughs went through. She knew that calves weren't the most well-mannered dinner companions one could ask for. And sweet as the hay smelled, she didn't think she'd care to tuck her newborn baby away in it—especially not if he were to be surrounded by hungry animals eagerly eyeing his mattress.

As Kara pondered this, she realized that Jesus, accustomed to all the glory of heaven, knew that these were the conditions He would be coming into. He knew His surroundings would be crude and that His first visitors would be a group of poor shepherds.

Kara realized, too, that Jesus knew all along He would face conditions far worse than those of the crude little Bethlehem stable. He knew from the beginning that He would hang on a cruel Roman cross and take upon Himself the sins of this wicked world.

What a sweet peace, Kara thought. *Jesus came willingly and peacefully into this sin-sick world, took my guilt upon Himself, and offers me that same sweet peace. How great His love is!*

Away in a
MANGER,
no crib for a bed,
The little Lord
JESUS
laid down His sweet head

The
STARS
in the sky
looked
DOWN
where He lay

The little
LORD JESUS,
asleep on the hay.

JOY
is like restless day;

PEACE
divine like quiet night.

ADELAIDE PROCTOR

But thou, Bethlehem Ephratah,
though thou be little among the
thousands of Judah,
yet out of thee shall he come forth
unto me that
is to be ruler in Israel;
whose goings forth
have been from of old,
from everlasting.

MICAH 5:2

GOODWILL

PEACE

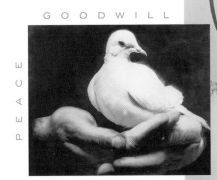

13

VOICES
in the MIST

The time draws near the birth of Christ:
The moon is hid; the night is still;
The Christmas bells from hill to hill
Answer each other in the mist.

Four voices of four hamlets round,
From far and near, on mead and moor,
Swell out and fail, as if a door
Were shut between me and the sound:

Each voice four changes on the wind,
That now dilate, and now decrease,
Peace and goodwill, goodwill and peace,
Peace and goodwill, to all mankind.

ALFRED, LORD TENNYSON

Of the increase of his government and peace
there shall be no end, upon the throne of David,
and upon his kingdom, to order it,
and to establish it with judgment and
with justice from henceforth even for ever.
The zeal of the LORD of hosts will perform this.

ISAIAH 9:7

It is "My own
PEACE I give you."
Not, notice,
the world's PEACE.

RUMER GODDEN

And in
HIS will
is our PEACE.

DANTE ALIGHIERI

EACE AND GOODWILL

BEHOLD
the
LAMB

Behold the Lamb of God,
which taketh away the sin of the world.

JOHN 1:29

There were two figures of shepherds near the stable. One was standing, staff in hand, the other was kneeling, a little lamb clutched in his grasp.

Perhaps, thought Kara, *the little lamb has become a pet to the young shepherd.* Kara remembered the sheep that her grandparents had kept on their little hobby farm. She had loved to watch the lambs bouncing around in the pasture. She thought back to the summer she had turned nine. There'd been a lamb that had lost its mama. Kara had promptly adopted the orphan and dubbed it "Snowflake." She'd helped to bottle-feed and otherwise care for her lamb, and she and Snowflake had been constant companions.

But our sheep were pretty much just for fun, Kara thought. *Once I claimed Snowflake as my own, I didn't have to give her up.*

Was that little shepherd clinging to his lamb in fear that he'd have to give him up for a Passover meal or burnt offering? After all, that's what his job was all about. Was he thinking of the angel's announcement, "Unto you is born this day in the city of David a Saviour, which is Christ the Lord"? Was he rejoicing in the peace that the angel had spoken of, knowing that even as he knelt there beside the manger, he was gazing at Jesus, God's perfect Lamb—the One who would be the ultimate sacrifice to pay the price for his sins?

Maybe, Kara reasoned, *just maybe the young shepherd realizes that the true peace he is searching for can be given to him by the tiny baby on a bed of hay.*

Hark!

The herald angels sing

GLORY to the newborn king

PEACE on earth, and mercy mild,

GOD and sinners reconciled!

CHARLES WESLEY

PEACE & GOODWILL

Therefore being
justified by FAITH,

we have PEACE
with God

through our
Lord JESUS Christ.

ROMANS 5:1

"PEACE on the earth,

good will to men,

From Heaven's all gracious King."

The world in solemn stillness lay,

To hear the angels sing.

EDMUND HAMILTON SEARS,
FROM "IT CAME UPON
THE MIDNIGHT CLEAR"

GOODWILL

PEACE

19

P E A C E

Peace was the first thing the angels sang.

Peace is the mark of the sons of God.

Peace is the nurse of love.

Peace is the mother of unity.

Peace is the rest of blessed souls.

Peace is the dwelling place of eternity.

LEO THE GREAT

These things I have spoken unto you, that in me ye might have peace. In the world ye shall have tribulation: but be of good cheer; I have overcome the world.

JOHN 16:33

For the mountains shall depart, and the hills be removed; but my kindness shall not depart from thee, neither shall the covenant of my peace be removed, saith the LORD that hath mercy on thee.

ISAIAH 54:10

PEACE & GOODWILL

JOURNEY to PEACE

Where is he that is born King of the Jews?
for we have seen his star in the east,
and are come to worship him.

MATTHEW 2:2

Three men in elegant clothing and carrying finely carved boxes completed the scene. Kara's pastor had once mentioned that there had probably been quite a few more wise men than the three normally mentioned. She figured this trio was just representative of the number of precious gifts mentioned in Matthew.

So how many wealthy, important men actually did leave their comfortable homes to follow an unusual star? mused Kara. *Did they even know for sure what they were looking for?*

Kara recalled that the wise men had asked Herod where the King of the Jews was to be born. She wondered why they would be so interested in the King of the Jews. Did they go searching for all newborn babies who were heirs to thrones? As she continued to ponder this, she began to realize that these men knew the Scriptures. They knew that this baby was much more than an earthly king; He was the promised Messiah—the Savior of the world.

That's why they could leave their comforts and follow a star to find a baby. God had fulfilled His promise to send the Messiah. Surely they could trust Him to lead them by His star.

Peace, thought Kara. *These men had every earthly pleasure they could possibly desire. What they were searching for was a true and lasting peace. They knew that would come only if they took the rough journey through the sand to find the King of the Jews—the only One capable of giving true and lasting peace.*

All men desire
PEACE,
but few
DESIRE the things
that make for
PEACE.

THOMAS À KEMPIS

And let the **PEACE** of God rule in your **HEARTS**,
to the which also ye are **CALLED** in one body;
and be ye **THANKFUL**.

COLOSSIANS 3:15

CHRISTMAS EVERYWHERE

Everywhere, everywhere, Christmas tonight!
Christmas in lands of the fir-tree and pine,
Christmas in lands of the palm-tree and vine,
Christmas where snow peaks stand solemn and
white, Christmas where cornfields stand sunny and
bright. Christmas where children are hopeful
and gay, Christmas where old men are patient
and gray, Christmas where peace, like a dove
in his flight, Broods o'er brave men in the thick
of the fight; Everywhere, everywhere, Christmas
tonight! For the Christ-child who comes is the Master
of all; No palace too great, no cottage too small.

PHILLIPS BROOKS

PEACE GOODWILL

PEACE

is always beautiful.

WALT WHITMAN

Now the Lord of **PEACE** himself
give you **PEACE** always by all means.
The **LORD** be with you all.

2 THESSALONIANS 3:16

God rest ye, little children;
let nothing you afright,
For Jesus Christ, your Savior,
was born this happy night;
Along the hills of Galilee
the white flocks sleeping lay,
When Christ,
the child of Nazareth,
was born on
Christmas day.

DINAH MULOCK CRAIK

GOODWILL

DEPART in PEACE

Lord, now lettest thou thy servant depart in peace,
according to thy word:
For mine eyes have seen thy salvation,
Which thou hast prepared
before the face of all people;
A light to lighten the Gentiles,
and the glory of thy people Israel.

LUKE 2:29–32

As Kara finished contemplating the holy scene before her, her thoughts shifted to a beautiful but often overlooked part of the Christmas story. In her mind she saw an old gentleman in Jerusalem who made regular treks to the temple to worship. She knew little about Simeon other than that he'd been promised by the Holy Spirit that he would not taste death before seeing the promised Messiah.

Of all of the thousands upon thousands of people waiting for Messiah, why would God have chosen to make this promise to Simeon? wondered Kara. *He must have had a deep and very personal relationship with his heavenly Father.*

Kara pulled her Bible from the coffee table in front of her and turned to the portion of Luke that contained this story. As she began reading, she thought of the great joy Simeon must have felt that day as he hurried to do the bidding of the Holy Spirit. She could almost feel the warmth of the smile on his wrinkled face as he pulled the child close and blessed the Lord.

"Lord, now lettest thou thy servant depart in peace." Kara whispered the words. Again she thought of the relationship Simeon must have had with God.

He was ready to die—even looking forward to it, thought Kara. *His great desire and only real need was to see the Lord's salvation. Once that happened, he was ready to meet God face-to-face.*

The reality of the story made Kara's heart beat a little faster as she realized how like Simeon everyone is. All we need is to see and accept the salvation of the Lord. Then we, too, can say, "Lettest thou thy servant depart in peace." What an awesome gift!

PEACE IS. . .

understanding the "oneness" OF GOD

and the "oneness" WITH GOD.

AUTHOR UNKNOWN

CHRISTMAS

is not a time nor a season,
but a STATE OF MIND.
To cherish PEACE
and GOODWILL,
to be plenteous in mercy,
is to have
the real spirit of CHRISTMAS.

CALVIN COOLIDGE

PEACE & GOODWILL

PEACE

is the deliberate adjustment
of my life to the will of God.

AUTHOR UNKNOWN

Thou wilt keep him in
perfect PEACE,
whose mind is stayed on thee:
because he trusteth in thee.

ISAIAH 26:3

Let us have
PEACE.

ULYSSES S. GRANT

GRACE and PEACE
be multiplied unto you through
the KNOWLEDGE of GOD,
and of JESUS our LORD.

2 PETER 1:2

PEACE

. . .is normally a great good, and normally coin-
cides with righteousness, but it is righteousness
and not peace which should bind the conscience
of a nation as it should bind the conscience of an
individual; and neither a nation nor an individual
can surrender conscience to another's keeping.

THEODORE ROOSEVELT

In the midst of all the hustle, bustle, and excitement of this holiday season, take time to pause and reflect upon the most precious gift of all—the gift of God's Son. Through Him you can know true and lasting peace—the kind only He can give. It is my prayer that you will be blessed with this abundant peace today and always.

For God so **LOVED** the **WORLD**,
that he gave his only begotten **SON**,
that whosoever
BELIEVETH in him
should not perish,
but have **EVERLASTING LIFE**.

JOHN 3:16

MERRY CHRISTMAS!